This Boxer Book belongs to

. . . .

www.boxerbooks.com

For Louis Frederick Van Liefland: may he laugh all his life
Kate Petty

With love to Val and Brian
Georgie Birkett

First published in Great Britain in 2008
by Boxer Books Limited.
www.boxerbooks.com

ISBN 13: 978-1-905417-16-2

1 3 5 7 9 10 8 6 4 2

Printed in China

Ha Ha, Baby!

Written by Kate Petty

Illustrated by Georgie Birkett

Boxer Books

Today, our baby is not laughing. Not a hint of a dimple or a glimmer of a smile, but a face like . . .

thunder!

"Oh, dear," said Ma. "I'll just try a little tickle on the tummy and another one on the toes."

"Tee hee, Baby!" laughed Ma.
But the baby just scowled.

In came Pa. "Today," said Ma, "our baby is **not laughing.**"

"Oh, dear," said Pa. "Not even the ghost of a grin?"

"Let's try the high stuff. Let's fly through the sky!

Whee! Whee!

Whee, Baby!"

laughed Pa. But the baby just glared.

In came Grandma.
"Today," said Ma and Pa,
"our baby is
not laughing."

"Deary me," said Grandma.
"No cheeky chuckling?

"Where's Grandma, Baby?
Peek-a-boo, here I am!
Boo, boo, Baby!"
laughed Grandma.
But the baby just turned away.

In came Grandpa. "Today," said Ma, Pa and
Grandma, "our baby is not laughing."

"Good grief!" said Grandpa.
"No burbling or gurgling?

"I'll blow some bubbles, Baby.
Watch me wave my wand.
Ho, ho, ho, Baby!"
laughed Grandpa.

But the baby just
harumphed!

The dog and the cat
each took a turn.
"Wow!" said the dog.

"Bow, wow!"

And he tried out his
tricks one by one . . .

"Purr, purr!"
purred the cat, rubbing her soft silky fur
against the baby. Then she chased her tail
round six times in a circle.

But our baby just yawned.

"Oh, dear!" wailed Ma and Pa and Grandma and Grandpa (and the cat and dog). "What shall we do now? Poor Baby, you must be so sad."

And they all gathered round and cooed at the baby.

"Waaaaaaaaaah!" cried the baby.

The baby made such a noise!
And that's when I came in.
"What's the matter?" I asked.

"Our baby isn't laughing today," they replied,
"and we don't know what to do."

"Perhaps the baby doesn't want to laugh today," I said. "Is that right, Baby?"

But the baby just **stared** at me.

"Two can play at that game," I said.
"Let's stare at each other for as long as we can . . .

and absolutely **no** laughing."

First with a dimple, then with a smile,
a ghost of a grin, a chuckle and a chortle . . .

a burble . . .

and a gurgle,

our baby
laughed . . .

. . . and laughed and laughed!

Other Boxer Books paperbacks

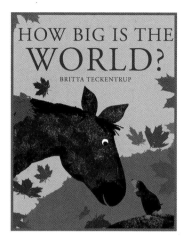

How Big is the World?: **Britta Teckentrup**

"How big is the world?" asked Little Mole.
"Why don't you go and find out?" replied papa.
Journey to the far corners of the world with
Little Mole, as he takes his first steps into a
wider world.
ISBN 13: 978-1-905417-62-9

Snail's Birthday Wish: **Fiona Rempt • Noëlle Smit**

It's Snail's birthday and all his friends have gathered
in the forest to celebrate. But can they make Snail's
greatest wish come true? This heartwarming tale
of friendship and fun that will be enjoyed by all.
ISBN 13: 978-1-905417-63-6

Boys Are Best!: **Manuela Olten**

"Boys are best! Girls are silly!"
"Girls are scared of everything!
They're even scared of ghosts…"
"Did you say ghosts?"
*'A book that should be on the shelf
in every child's room – both girls and boys.'*
SAARBRUCKER ZEITUNG
ISBN 13: 978-1-905417-66-7